GET A MOVE ON!

BEN BAILEY SMITH

ILLUSTRATED BY METTE ENGELL

BLOOMSBURY EDUCATION

LONDON   OXFORD   NEW YORK   NEW DELHI   SYDNEY

BLOOMSBURY EDUCATION
Bloomsbury Publishing Plc
50 Bedford Square, London, WC1B 3DP, UK

BLOOMSBURY, BLOOMSBURY EDUCATION and the Diana logo
are trademarks of Bloomsbury Publishing Plc

First published in Great Britain in 2019 by Bloomsbury Publishing Plc

A catalogue record for this book is available from the British Library

ISBN: PB: 978-1-4729-6122-8; ePDF: 978-1-4729-6121-1; ePub: 978-1-4729-6120-4;
enhanced ePub: 978-1-4729-6954-5

2 4 6 8 10 9 7 5 3 1

Printed and bound in China by Leo Paper Products, Heshan, Guangdong

To find out more about our authors and books visit www.bloomsbury.com
and sign up for our newsletters

"Get a move on!
No more slacking!
Action stations!
Let's get cracking!"

Mum is shouting in that mum way;
Let me guess, it must be Monday.

"Up you get, Max!" Daddy roars;
Eve's already up of course.
Bet he'll say before we leave:
"Why can't you be more like Eve?"

"Why can't you be more like Eve?"
He says, and then, "What's on my sleeve?!"

"That looks like a ketchup stain…
Hard to wash out," I explain.

Daddy screams and disappears
And Pep decides to lick my ears.
I tickle his chin and then:
"MAX, I WON'T TELL
YOU AGAIN!"

Mum yells, "Have you seen the clock?!"

Dad shouts, "WHERE'S MY YELLOW SOCK?!"

I put on a puppet show.
(Pep's a little busy though.)

"Oh this is beyond belief,"
Says Dad, and Mum shouts, "Brush
your teeth!"
Think I'll do it AFTER toast.
It makes the marmalade taste gross.

Mummy shouts, "I'll
go bananas
If you're still in your
pyjamas!"

Daddy's face goes stiff and shaky
When I show him Mr Snakey.

Eve is washing up her plate
And says, "Hey, Mum, it's getting late."

Mummy goes to start the car
And I look for that orange jar.

Just then I hear,
"Martin, MARTIN!
Come outside,
the car's not
starting!"

18

"That's a shame," I start to say,
"And Eve's Big School's quite far away."
Eve just glares and folds her arms
And Dad screams,
"JUST KEEP CALM,
KEEP CALM!"

He trips on a
tennis racquet
And tears a bit
of his jacket.

Dad goes out and Mum comes in,
Eve's eyes roll round in a spin.

On the window I show Pep
How to draw by using breath.

Mum has some
leaves in her hair,

Dad makes
noises like
a bear.

Eve says, "Mother! Make a call
And tell them I'll be late for school!"

"Better do the same for work,"
Says Mum, then, "What's that on
your shirt?"

"Oh for Pete's sake!" Dad says after.
"Who's Pete?" I ask. No one
answers.

I turn to the glass and spy
Someone I know passing by
Through the window, walking right past,
Kate McKenzie! She's in my class.

I knock on the glass and wave. Kate waves back and smiles and waits.

Kate is always fun to talk to.
Her mum calls out, "We can
walk you!"

"Yay!" I shout, give Pep a stroke
And go and get my bag and coat.
Grab my scarf and just before
I go to walk out through the door,

29

I turn to say goodbye to Mum
And Dad and Eve, but everyone
Is shouting, screaming, making calls,
Black stuff's dripping in the hall.

I don't think they've read the time.
"Guys it's nearly ten to nine!
I'm walking to school with Kate."

"Get a move on!
You'll be late!"